I Think
I Think a Lot

Jessica Whipple

Illustrated by Josée Bisaillon

free spirit
PUBLISHING®

This book has been filed with the Library of Congress.
LCCN: 2023001811

Free Spirit Publishing does not have control over or assume responsibility for author or third-party websites and their content. At the time of this book's publication, all facts and figures cited within are the most current available. All telephone numbers, addresses, and website URLs are accurate and active; all publications, organizations, websites, and other resources exist as described in this book; and all have been verified as of April 2023. If you find an error or believe that a resource listed here is not as described, please contact Free Spirit Publishing. Parents, teachers, and other adults: We strongly urge you to monitor children's use of the internet.

Edited by Cassie Sitzman
Cover and interior design by Courtenay Fletcher

Printed in China

Free Spirit Publishing
An imprint of Teacher Created Materials
9850 51st Avenue North, Suite 100
Minneapolis, MN 55442
(612) 338-2068
help4kids@freespirit.com
freespirit.com

To my parents.
—J.W.

To my younger self.
—J.B.

I think.

I think a lot.

I think I think a lot.

More than most other kids.

I know this because of Caleb.

When he paints his pinch pot,
his brush is quick and confident,
like he's conducting an orchestra
and it's the fast part.

I wonder if he's been planning it out all morning.
Does he worry about getting it just right,
like I do?

I paint slowly.

What colors
should I use?

Do I have everything
I need?

What if I make
a mistake?

But a thunderstorm is slow too.

It rolls along, gathering clouds, energy,
before drenching everything in a fresh, even coat of wet.

When I paint,
I paint like a thunderstorm,
to be sure I've covered all
the bare spots.

I think a lot.
More than most other kids.

I know this because of Ana.

When she apologizes,
SORRY
spurts from her mouth
like water from the
lunchroom fountain.

Ana's off to play again
before those two syllables
have fully left her lips.

No one else seems to use as many words as I do.
They don't have to get them all out,
like me.

That's because there's a lot I wonder about.

Did I hurt her feelings?
Is she mad at me?

Is she OKAY?
IS SHE MAD?
Im sorry!

What if I'm not a good friend?

But a book uses a lot of words.

Sometimes thousands,
    or millions,
filling zillions of pages,
    making pictures with each phrase.

When I say sorry,
it's like I'm writing a story
with lots of details,
so the other person knows
their feelings matter to me.

I think a lot.
More than most other kids.

I know this because of Emory.

When there are cupcakes,
Emory eats one,
then another,
as if they come in pairs,
like cherries do.

He doesn't say thank you
for the second one.
He's busy having fun.

I wonder if he worries about seeming greedy.
Do his thoughts ever spoil the fun,
like mine do?

THANK YOU! thanks!

So sometimes
I repeat myself.

THANK YOU AGAIN!

Did they hear me?
Thank you.

Did I sound like
I meant it?
THANK YOU!

I should smile.
Thank you!

But a bird repeats itself.

It makes the same call
over and over,
sharing gratitude with friends
for the glories of the morning.

When I'm grateful, I'm a bird.

I repeat my thanks because
I want the person to know
—really know—
that I'm glad for what they've given me.

I think a lot.
More than most other kids.

I know I do.

Because sometimes my thoughts turn into worries.
And sometimes they won't leave me alone.

But there's a good part:
I care a lot!

About being kind,

about doing good work,

about showing I'm grateful,
about other people's feelings.

I care a lot.

Not more than other kids,
just in my own way.

Because I want to be good . . .

...at being **ME.**

A Note from the Author

I wrote this story about a girl like me—a girl with obsessive-compulsive disorder, or OCD. People often think OCD is all about obsessive cleanliness, and sometimes it is. But a person with OCD can have obsessions and compulsions about many other things. I was obsessed with "being good."

To me, that meant showing concern for people's feelings, being kind and polite, and being careful. These are all wonderful things, and people often strive for these attributes. But I felt extreme distress if I believed I wasn't living up to standard. I got upset when I made a mistake. I would think for days, over and over, about every minor infraction. If I didn't think I was "good," I didn't think I was okay.

I wrote this book to share a bit of my own experience, but I chose not to dwell on suffering. Instead, I wanted to share a discovery: **sometimes on the underside of suffering, you can find something beautiful.** My hope is that many children, especially those who struggle with anxiety or overthinking, can see themselves in these pages and make that discovery for themselves.

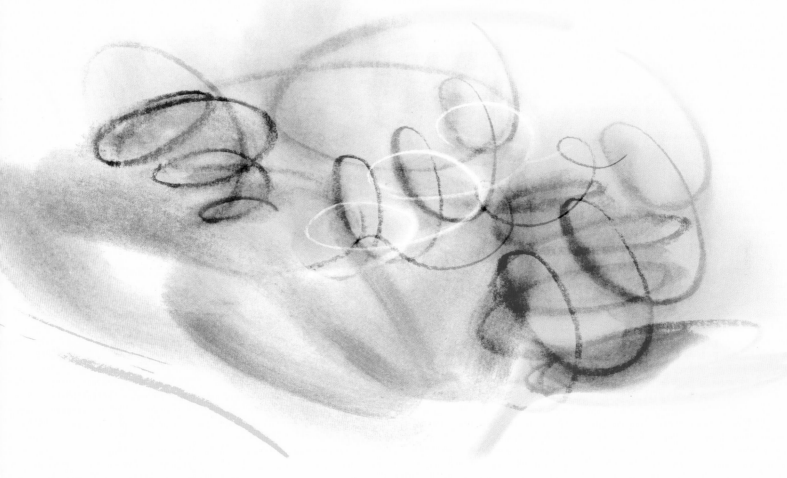

Sharing this book can help. Reading it together can be a way to open a conversation about anxious or worried thoughts, thoughts that seem stuck, or thoughts *that just won't leave the child alone*. It can also open the door to discussions about overthinking, comparison, and perfectionism. Sharing this book can help children grow empathy and understanding for other people's experiences and ways of thinking and being in the world.

Thank you for reading *I Think I Think a Lot* with children and connecting with my story. I hope it—and the conversations you might have as a result—will be helpful for the worried or overthinking child in your life, no matter the origin of that anxiety. The questions on the next page can serve as a guide for talking with children about the book's themes.

Discussing the Story

Worry and Anxiety

- Do you ever worry? What do you worry about? What does worry feel like for you?

- When you feel worried, what helps you feel better?

- Talking about worries can help them feel less overwhelming. Who are some adults you can talk to?

Discovering the Good

- Think of a time when something good happened because of something troubling. What happened?

- Think of a time when you had to do something difficult. What is one good thing that came as a result?

- What do you like about yourself?

Empathy and Understanding

- Are there ways that you are similar to the main character in this book? How are you different?

- Think about one of your friends. What are some things that come easily to you? What are some things your friend excels at? How do you feel about these differences?

- How could you help someone who is worried?

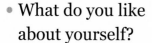

A Note About OCD

OCD is an anxiety disorder that's characterized by bothersome and unwanted thoughts/feelings (called obsessions) and actions performed to relieve the distress from those thoughts/feelings (called compulsions). These obsessions and compulsions are time-consuming, cause the person extreme distress, and get in the way of important things in their life. This book is not meant to diagnose or treat OCD. If you believe your child might be suffering from OCD, reach out to your pediatrician or a qualified therapist. You can find a list of therapists who specialize in working with people with OCD, as well as OCD information and resources, at the International OCD Foundation website (iocdf.org).

About the Author and Illustrator

© Nick Gould

Jessica Whipple (authorjessicawhipple.com) is a writer for adults and children. She is the author of *Enough Is . . .* (Tilbury House) and *I Think I Think a Lot*. Her poetry has been published in print and online literary magazines. When she's not tinkering with words, Jessica loves to create with anything else she can get her hands on. She has refinished antique dining chairs, crocheted sweaters, designed and built miniature mouse houses, and once hoarded a mess of zebra grass with the hopes of making a wreath. Jessica lives with her family in Eastern Pennsylvania. To read more of her work, visit her website or follow @JessicaWhippl17 on Twitter.

As a young girl, **Josée Bisaillon** loved drawing cats and houses. She really enjoyed school and always returned home full of stories to tell. She liked being in the classroom so much that she pursued her education all the way to university, where she studied graphic design. It was there that she fell in love with illustration. Since 2005, with scissors and brushes in hand, Josée has illustrated more than forty children's books, as well as magazines and newspapers for adults. Josée lives just outside of Montreal with her spouse, their three children, one hairless cat, and many paper characters.

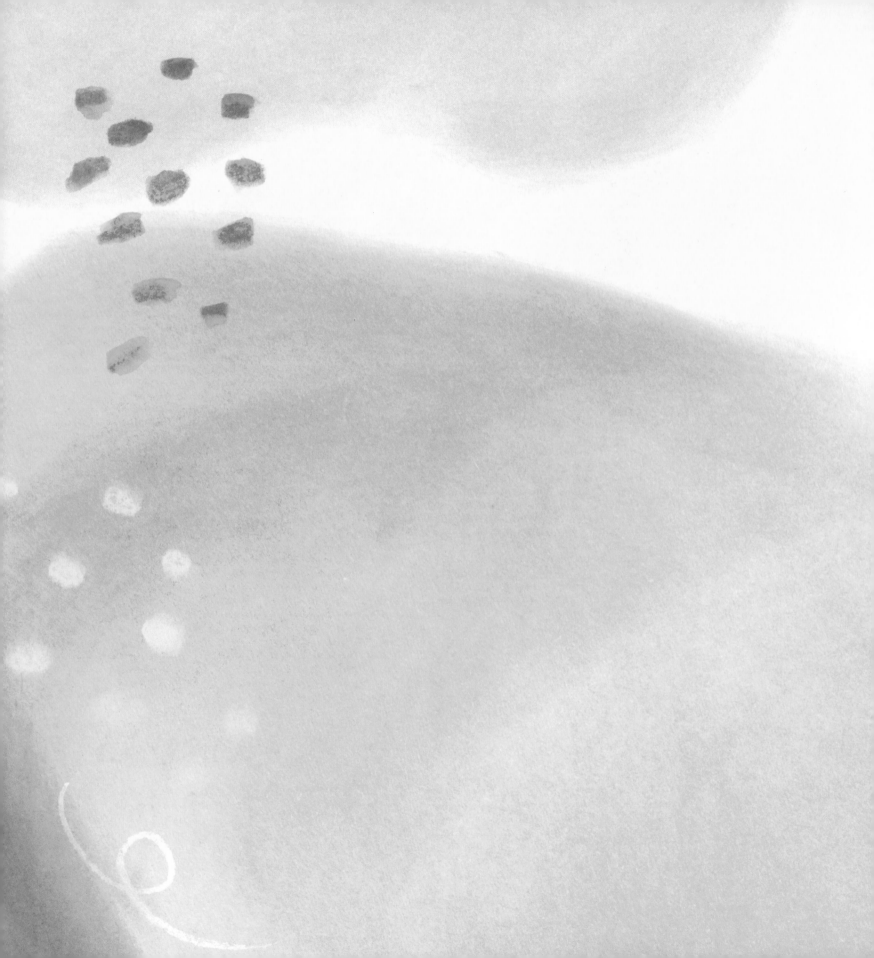